Deep Minds Anonymous

Madiha Batool

Copyright © 2017 Madiha Batool

All rights reserved.

ISBN:
ISBN: 9781549932427

DEDICATION

I would like to dedicate this book to my parents, because of whom I am standing here today. They have supported me in all my life quests and everything that I have ever believed in. Also, to achieve any success in life, one needs someone to be by their side no matter what and for that I would like dedicate this book to my sister as well who has always been my backbone in all phases of life, pushing me to do more and always encouraging me to fulfill my dreams.

CONTENTS

	Acknowledgments	I
1	The Beauty Of A Goddess	Pg # 1
2	A Glimpse To The Window Of My Soul	Pg # 40
3	Rise From The Ashes	Pg # 82
4	Deep Thoughts and Feelings	Pg # 103

ACKNOWLEDGMENTS

I would like to express my ample gratitude to my family, I don't know how I would have made it this far without their support and motivation. And to my friends for always having faith in me and encouraging me to reach my potential. Also, to my loving sister who always believed in me and had faith in me.

1 THE BEAUTY OF A GODDESS

She is a wild one with a heart
that never hardens,
a soul that cannot be tamed.
She's a goddess who with all her
might can turn pain into power
and every thorn into a flower.

A mind so deep,
a soul so pure
and a heart made of gold.
She is a woman who loves
beyond measure and asks for nothing
but only love in return.

Her soul is tired from fighting against the
insecurities she is forced to feel in her heart,
in spite of her rare self that shines inside out.
But, she has a warrior's heart with a beautiful soul,
who can spellbound you in no time,
not with her outer beauty but with her mesmerizing aura
and when she will open her mouth to speak, you'd be hung
up on the magic in her every word.

Her eyes are the size of the moon,
once you look into them,
there is no coming out without falling deeply in love.

Her wild side showed
her inner beauty as it shined
through her gypsy soul.
She's a beautiful goddess of nature,
wilderness and mother earth.

Her red hair is
as wild as a lioness
with rebel in her soul
and fire in her eyes.
She is no less than a force
to be reckoned with.

Her smile was the only ornament she needed
to wear to look absolutely stunning,
stealing hearts everywhere she went.
But, her heart was waiting for the one who'd
dare to look more deeply in her eyes and find
the pain she had hidden
behind her beautiful smile.

She feels at peace while sitting by
the fresh soil of earth where
nature blooms in all forms; freshly cut grass,
enchanting green trees standing tall and firm
on the ground, dazzling flowers
blossoming in the fall.
She feels as if her soul is at home
With nature all around her.

Her life was the most beautiful story
I've ever laid my eyes on.
All I ever wanted was to read
each and every page of it,
till I would fall in love all parts of her
whether good or bad, every intricate
detail made her even more beautiful.

She has a mind of her own,
with thoughts running wild,
carelessly tripping on all the memories
she'd rather not think of.
It's hard for her to give a rest to these
unwanted thoughts about what might
have been, as it's all she had ever dreamed of.
But, this October; it's time to
let the dead leaves drop
and to dream new dreams.

She has always been a lone wolf
among the sheep, blazing her own trail
behind for others to learn.
She has always had to carve her own path
which was dangerously hers and hers alone.

She is a beautiful masterpiece of chaos
and mess underneath her perfect exterior.
But, she gets even more magical
when she embraces her imperfections
as her perfections and is just herself.

She is a beautiful soul who loves
too deep and thinks too much.
I think that is why she is broken
because she loves from the depth of her heart
but doesn't always get the love she deserves.

She is a beautiful mosaic of all the fragments
of her broken heart that she gave out to those
whom she had ever loved, maybe that is why she
always feels so incomplete because anyone who
left, took away a piece with them,
leaving a permanent scar.

Her mind dwells in a secretive place,
quite mysterious to the thoughtless
people on and about her.
She is like a flower as beautiful as a magnolia
that blossoms in late spring.
Let her bloom, shine and enchant the world
that is lucky enough to bend their gaze upon her.

She is a wild child
with a gypsy soul
that dances with the stars.
She has a free spirit,
a reckless mind and a rebel heart
that isn't meant to be tamed.
Love her wild and
you will never lose her.

She is a beauty behind those scars,
She is a gorgeous chaos underneath all that mess,
She is everything that you can't see,
Because her beauty lies deep within,
Simply, look into her eyes and see her soul.

She is a living proof that beauty has
nothing to do with appearances;
it's evident in the way her beauty
shines from the inside out,
the way her eyes dance when she laughs,
the way she loves every living soul,
even though her heart was brutally broken
and innocently walks on earth
like an angel in disguise.

She is a rose without a thorn,
she has magic in her eyes,
fire in her soul,
and love in her bones.

She is a magnificent creature with both;
intense love and hate in her heart.
Treat her right and she will let her guard
down by loving you fiercely,
but dare to do her wrong
and you shall know
how beastly a beauty can be.

She is an angel with a heart of gold
and a warrior's spirit within her.
But, don't get her wrong,
she can disguise as a devil
when forced to walk
in the midst of fire.

She was rain in all her essence and purity,
she danced to the rhythm of her heart,
laughed with beauty and grace.
No wonder he lost his heart
while dancing in the rain.

Her tear stained cheeks told
a completely different story.
Nobody could ever know
that she was the same girl who
stood bravely like a queen,
greeting the war of life
each day with a smile.

She is made of stardust and magic.
She carries heavens burden on her wings like shoulders.
She is a walking contradiction with fire and ice in her soul.

She is stronger than you think.
But, her heart has been walked on so many
times that she no longer lets her guard down
for anyone to dare to love her.
So when she sets her fears aside,
and opens her heart for you,
treasure and cherish her because
brave souls like her are hard to find.

She isn't just beautiful,
she is a lion hearted girl with a poetic soul.
she is my muse, my flame.

All the adjectives in the world could not
do justice to the beauty that she was.

She is out of the ordinary,
not knowing in her wildest imagination
what the future beholds,
yet dreaming and weaving hopes
of living her fairy tale.

She only wanted love from a man
who wasn't afraid to accept her
as she was; flaws and all.
Every second her heart skipped a beat
and lurched for someone
to look at her as poetry
and love her for eternity.

She is the type of girl who
believes in the magic of words
as her life surrounds around
the beauty of poetry.
She is just an incurable dreamer
and a hopeful romantic.

She wanted to bury her head
in the world of books and poetry,
disappearing and completely vanishing
in the wild imagination of her mind.

She was like a diamond;
rough at the surface, sharp at the edges
yet immensely beautiful, sparkling
like the dancing of new stars.
No matter how hard he'd try,
he couldn't look away,
staring in her ocean like eyes;
he fell deeper and deeper in love.

She was the brightest one in the dark,
shining with the glow of her stardust soul,
like a moon child who only
shined brightest in the dark.

Her beauty and her brain together made
her irresistible. It's no wonder that
countless men have fallen victims
to her wit and magical charm.
Yet she awaits the one who'll
fall in love with her naked soul.

Unlock her caged heart and really love every
inch of her and she will give her all to you;
every piece of her soul and
every little bit of her heart.

Dear Men,

When she tells you little things about her,
pay attention and listen to all she has to say.
There is beauty hidden in her
spoken words and those left unsaid.
Listen with the intent to understand her,
and you'll be soon falling in love
with the magic that she is.

She loves to dance in the rain,
she enjoys walking barefoot on the beach,
the feeling of sand between her toes gives her joy,
and she is full of sunshine and love.
In a nutshell,
she is simply a beautiful present of life,
silently waiting to be unwrapped.

She longs for nights filled with
moonlight, adventure and passion.
She is a wanderer of the night;
a lover of all wild things.

She is both; a little bit of the devil
and a little bit of an angel.
She's the kind that
makes you want to sin
just as she makes your knees go weak
and fall for the saintly devil she is.

2 A GLIMPSE TO THE WINDOW OF MY SOUL

My poetry is a glimpse to the window of my soul.
My words sing of my struggle and hardship,
just as they applaud my courage of enduring life.
I write them as raw as they come
to truly express my pain and heal.
Words have that power
you know; they can even cure
the deepest of cuts.

Your words are music to my soul.
They make me want to dance
and love with the intensity
of a thousand suns.
Talk to me like rain
and let me dance in it.

Poetry is a cure for me;
it crawls deeply into the darkest corners
of my soul and slowly and gently heals.
It speaks the unspoken words that
explain how bad it hurts.

The moon and I share
a love so deep
that I faithfully see him
night after night,
anxiously waiting for
the day to pass
and the sun to set.

The ache of lost love
never goes away.
As time goes by,
we only learn to
live with the pain
and keep it buried deep
inside our broken hearts
forever till the end of time.

Simple things are beautiful and unique
because their beauty is hidden deep within.
Look with the eyes of your soul and you'll
find that what's inside is what truly matters.

A poet is the one who becomes a voice
for the silent, yet frantically beating heart.

My beauty is more than skin deep.
Touch me with your words where your
hands can't reach and make love to my soul.

Loving someone and losing yourself in the
process means going to war every day,
breaking on the inside.
Nobody knows of the battles you
are fighting in your heart.
At the end of it all, you either come
out the other side or you don't.

When you say you love me, show me that you care,
hold me in the darkness and love me for my dark.

She got Goosebumps,
as she felt a shiver down her spine,
and with the preparations of Halloween
in full swing, even the air she breathed in,
had devilish enchantment written all over it.
It was fate that the voice from the past spoke,
turning her troubled mind to the chapter
of the past ghosts tormenting her;
digging up a grave for her to lie in.
But, the soul that lay within her
was indestructible, and in the midst of the spirit
of Halloween, the evil force got its match;
as she chose to burn all grief-stricken memories
and held nothing back, only love and light.

My poetry explains the words I fail to speak.

This sadness in me crawls into the darkest corners
of my soul, and hides where my demons abide.
Come closer, run your fingers over the cracks
in my heart and fill them up with your love.

Poetry is as beautiful as it's painful,
they are words felt, not thought of.
Something so rarely expressed,
something that is left unsaid,
something that could be utterly
mesmerizing or destructive,
something that's been kept inside for too long,
It either breaks one apart or heals the broken heart.

Loving you was hard but it wasn't as hard
as trying to love with this broken heart again.

Love me like you would love
your own shadow.
Love me like I am the only person
left in the universe for you,
Love me like you couldn't bear to be torn
apart from me for a second,
Love me like I am your most beautiful mistake,
your darkest sin, one you'd commit over and over again.

In the abyss of loneliness,
the tears that I have shed,
the pain that I have endured was
more than I thought I could take.
But, I found the strength within me
in the horrors of dark.
I found myself in the beauty of it
and that I was the light
inside all the darkness.

My soul aches for the sweet
touch of your soul,
meet me in the abyss of my darkness
and save me from the dark.

Madiha Batool

And so,
in the dark hours
of the night,
I let my guard down.
I let myself be.
All that I do and feel
stays a secret between
the moon and me.

He was looking for a soul
who'd know how to
calm the chaos in his heart
and silence his demons
which were forever yearning to
dance with somebody in the moonlight.

His words stole my heart and by a fraction of a second,
I was lost and blind in love with the beauty of his soul.

For her entire life,
she dreamt of the perfect things to
encounter her; not knowing that nothing
is perfect. It's what seems perfect to the eyes, because
sometimes the most flawed and imperfect captures the
heart in the blink of an eye.

As her lips faked a smile,
her face drowned in her own ocean of tears,
as everyday she struggled to move on,
she tripped and fell,
but didn't give up
and fearlessly continued down
the dark road as giving up
wasn't even an option.

And when are sitting alone in the dark,
I hope you remember all the
beautiful moments we shared,
And all the times I was there to hold you
so you don't fall apart,
I hope you remember how I loved your
imperfections more than your perfection.
I hope you remember that this broken heart
of mine will always love you with all its pieces.

The beauty in your heart
reflects through your eyes.
My darling,
the sun rises
and sets with you.
You are my muse,
my flame,
my love in my soul.

Deep Minds Anonymous

Like the ocean she was always
in deep thoughts as her mind
ran a thousand miles a minute;
relentless flashbacks of what was
and what would never be again.
Her heart ached at her misery
but her lips smiled as for another day,
she put on a fake face for the world.

He is a courageous knight in shining armor
with a poet's heart and a warrior's soul.
All he desires is a soul connection
with someone who'd love him
for his battle scars and
cracks in his armor.

And when it rains,
everything surrounding becomes bliss,
as if it purifies everything it touches.
The world gets blurred and
all you can see is beauty around you.
So when it rains, simply dance,
drain all your sorrows,
and let rain steal away the pain.

I will tear down my walls for you tonight,
if only you'd come a little closer,
run your fingers over the cracks of my heart
and love me like there is no tomorrow.

My heart is bleeding poetry tonight,
just as ink is bleeding of my pain.
So I write, unleashing my feelings on paper
so my heart feels lighter with every word.

And so, in the depths of despair,
I found only a ghost of you beside me
when what I needed was a hand to hold me
and tell me that it was all going to be okay
soon but all I got was silence in answer.
And that was the moment I knew
I had to be my own savior to
save me from the dark.

Poetry comes from the soul
to soothe the troubled mind.
As the mind wanders to seek answers;
unable to quench the thirst of deep insight,
roaming in absolute solitary,
comes to the finding that all one
seeks already resides within one,
always have and always will.
All you need to do is to look
with the eyes of your heart.

We were living in a dream,
You and I.
It shattered to pieces
and so did our hearts.
How vulnerable and fragile
are human's hearts with
little ray of hope that could
disappear in a heartbeat.

The beauty in her eyes
was utterly captivating,
they shined ever so brightly
like stars in a dark night.
The love in her heart
was the light of her rare self
which reflected through her soul.
All she wanted was soul recognition
with someone who'd look under the
surface and love her for who she was.
Someone who'd make love to her scars,
her freckles and would gently
lay his hand on her wounded heart.
Someone who'd make her
forget it was ever broken.

And just when our eyes locked;
it was as if electricity was trapped
between two souls.
I could feel the world stopping
only to let us have our moment
and I believe in that very second;
our souls were connected
and we were infinite.

He is a mysterious man
with eyes of a gambler
and mind of an evil genius
who ironically gambles
with everything, except love.
He's everything that he doesn't reveal;
a kind soul in disguise of the devil.

Her: Why am I attracted to bad men?
Him: Because you are too good for them and you think that the goodness of your heart might change them. You feel that their toughness is only a deceptive exterior, but in fact they are soft on the inside. And that if you break their walls, they'll let you in and you'll find their inner child that is loving and kind.

But, you see, not all bad men hide their goodness inside; most of them are who they show they are. Don't deceive yourself by believing there is good in everyone because there not always is. However, we all have good and bad in us. Try falling in love with everything about a person, beautiful and ugly parts of them and you'll never fall out of love with them.

My words tell the story of my heartache,
my struggle and my pain.
But most of all, it speaks of me conquering
over every dark thing that came my way.
I came out even stronger than before.

Madiha Batool

Falling in love with you broke my heart more
than anything ever did. But I'd break it
over and over again only to be consumed
by feelings of *you*.

Be with me in my darkest hour like a moon that
never leaves the sky even in the darkest of nights.

Touch and caress my bruised heart with your words,
and all those places where your hands can't reach.

The worst kind of pain is which you
keep buried inside and don't let anyone
know about it. You have a quiet
funeral for it in your heart and
let the tears dry on their own
for the fear that it may cause
grief to the ones you love.
The kind of pain that
can have no words.

3 RISE FROM THE ASHES

Rise from the ashes of your own life.
Don't let any defeat define
the rest of your story.
Don't let the fire die in your heart.
Be like the phoenix,
rise up from the ashes and soar.

Darling, you are no less than anyone else.
Don't let anyone make you feel less about
yourself because you are so much more.
Rise like a sun and shine like a moon
which enlightens the universe with
the beauty of its light.

You are far more unique than you know.
Don't ever let your potential go waste.
This world needs
your talent,
your story
and your vision.
You alone can change the world
if only you would believe in yourself like I do.

A single thread of hope sometimes could
bring so many possibilities in your life
that you could never have dreamt of.
Life changes drastically in small moments
and turns a beautiful page in your life,
leaving you in wonder at fate's power.
Never lose hope,
ever.

In a society that forces you to
wear a label wherever you go;
the only way to stay sane and
be the real you is to go rebel.
You don't need a label to define you;
it's you who gets to decide
what defines you.

If the world wounds your wings,
heal them till they shine bright again.
Don't let anyone stop you from
spreading your wings.
Fly to the sky and never
doubt yourself again

This world is at times too dark
too dreary to let light in,
but good always finds its way in
to enlighten where needed.
Don't be afraid of the dark,
sometimes you need to fall down a
deep hole to get to your wonderland.

This world needs more of who you are,
your authenticity, your passion,
your drive to make a difference in
the world makes you *you*.
Don't be afraid to think out of the box
or be the odd one out.
It is you that will change the world
one day by being true to yourself.

I see only beauty in your broken wings;
it's a proof of your courage that you
once deeply loved but were broken.
Lift your spirit brave angel,
you are worthy of flying with eagles
and never looking down again.

Sometimes, you need to walk through the shadows of darkness to truly appreciate the value of beauty and light.

There is so much beauty in your heart
that it reflects through your eyes
and shines through your soul.
You don't need the mirror telling
you how beautiful you look because
you see, beauty is not in the face,
but it is a light in your heart and soul.
If you are beautiful on the inside,
your inner beauty will shine through.

Do what makes your soul shine and light up the dark with your kindness, love and compassion.

Life doesn't always come as easy as we all want,
that is what makes it worth a while to take
up challenges wherever we can find them.
Don't be afraid to still be a learner,
there are many on this earth that walk proudly
being ignorant, you are lucky to be unlike them.
Seek and question,
there is beauty and wisdom in this world
if only you have the eyes to see it.

Life is but an echo of our memories,
moment's well spent and
unconditional love which conquers all.
So love deeply and live passionately
with no regrets, so that you greet death with a smile.

Hearts are meant to be broken.
It's as simple as that and even if you protect,
seal and conceal it behind your chest,
it will break no matter what.
Then why are you so afraid to live
and take your chances? Just live and love
with all your heart and if fate has written for you
a broken heart, love all the same and you will find
the one who can mend it by giving you the broken piece.

Don't look for a perfect person
because there is no such thing as perfect.
There is exquisite beauty in being
flawed and imperfect because the way
I see it, diamonds are full of edges
and yet, they shine forever.

I hope you know you are amazing just the way you are.
If not, let your scars tell the story of your bravery,
your broken heart the story of your courage,
and let the love in your heart be
the light of this world.
You see, all brave souls
have been scarred and broken and yet,
they never stopped being just who they are.

If you want love,
look inside your heart
where it is ever flowing.
If you want kindness,
be kind to strangers.
If you desire to be whole,
don't look for your other half to complete you,
because to be whole is to be complete within yourself.

Chase your dreams just as
kids chase kites flying in the sky.
Our dreams keep us
alive and lit a fire in our hearts,
pushing us to do more than just exist.
Fly with your dreams and
soar like an eagle.

Don't be a slave to anyone.
Be in charge of your mind and soul
because this world and it's people hold onto
every opportunity to control and manipulate you.
Be the artist of your life and paint your dreams
across all the skies of universe.
And to hell with what will people say because
their tongues never get tired of saying things anyway.
Be a fearless dreamer.

To all of you brave hearts;
my heart goes out for you.
In a world that is falling to pieces every day,
to keep on going in spite of everything
happening around you requires
courage and a brave soul.
Channel your pain into fuel,
keep fighting and never give up.

4 DEEP THOUGHTS AND FEELINGS

To be lonely is to be alone with
one's thoughts and emotions.
Only the one who isn't afraid of their own
mind and soul can find peace in loneliness.
It's easier said than done, because I know
the lonely dark hour too well.
So, the next time you feel lonely,
just come under the night sky,
gaze at the moon and the stars
and you'll know that you are not alone.
We are the scattered gazers of this universe,
linked together by the moon and the stars.

The irony of love is that no matter
how much it hurts, we never stop searching
for its existence to fill the empty void in our hearts.

Deep Minds Anonymous

I am a dreamer of dreams,
trying not to drown in a world
that is full of cruel and bitter things.

Love me for who I am, flaws and all.
My imperfections and faults
make me who I really am.
If you can't appreciate the beauty
in my rough edges, then you sure
as hell won't appreciate my good
amongst all the bad parts of me.

Even when you feel pain,
be happy that you are able
to feel something because for me
as a deeply feeling person,
there is nothing worse
than feeling numb.

I had to learn the hard way not to let anyone
touch my heart or come closer to me,
not because it has been broken before but
because I don't think I could heal myself
and repair the fragmented pieces
of my soul once again.

I never wanted a forever love
because I know nothing lasts forever,
all I ever wanted were your now's;
so that we could create a life
in our beautiful present.

And just when I thought I was finally happy,
I could hear my heart breaking open.
I wish I hadn't allowed joy and love to
enter my heart again when the world
we live in is filled with broken dreams
and everything in it comes with
an expiration date.

I hope one day the world finds
a way to fill up the cracks,
to mend broken hearts
and to give endless joy to those in pain.
I hope for a world where kindness exists,
and love overcomes the love of power.

The beauty of nature
and wilderness soothes my soul,
cleanses the mind
and calms the spirit.
And it's only there where
by losing yourself in the beauty of it,
will you truly find yourself.

I like the stillness of the night
when quietness creeps in,
darkness floods the room
and silence broods.
That's when I can be
unapologetically me.

I love to read because it takes me to a place
that is free from the reality of our lives.
It frees my soul and lets my imagination fly.

This world is filled with angels with
broken wings and demons with happy faces.
Be careful to choose who walks with you,
some people have become too good at lying.

I have been hurt
and betrayed more times
than I can count;
so it was the hard way
that I finally learned to trust
nobody but me.

Deep Minds Anonymous

I crave a deep soul connection
with someone who'd listen
to the whispers of my heart
and the things I have to say
even when no words
left my mouth.

.

Sometimes our mouths
don't match our hearts.
The words left unsaid
stay with us forever like
unfulfilled wishes drowning
under the anxiety of
what will people think.

I want it all or nothing.
I can never be content at heart
getting the half-ass of anything.
So love me whole or do not love me at all.

I want to live the life of a hippie
who doesn't live by the clock
and isn't bounded by time.
I want to live freely and
go where my heart desires,
I want to be boundless and infinite.

Life is hard enough already without
all the hypocrites pretending to be
what they are not. Their talk is
as sweet as honey while stabbing
you as your back is turned.
Too bad some people have become
too good at following such crowd
blindly, I've never been one to
kiss ass and never will.

Wishfulness runs in my veins;
a yearning that somebody someday
would dare to understand
the depth of my thoughts and
the incomprehensible mystery
that lies within my eyes.

I was daunted by the fact that here
I was breaking apart and you were
as silent as the grave.
That's when I learned that
at the end of the day,
we all have to pick our broken pieces
ourselves because everybody's busy
saving themselves.

Deep in my heart,
I know I am an old soul
caged in a young body,
who believes in poetry,
romance and all things
that make me feel alive
in this chaotic world.

Sometimes, we only fall in love
with being in love.
There's nothing our heart won't endure
only to be wanted and deeply loved.
Despite of all the heartbreak and pain,
we still look for love to heal in all the
places we've been hurt before.

I have sinned and repented.
I have been betrayed and hurt.
I have been through the halls of darkness
and yet I am standing in the shadow of light.
You can hate me, frown at me for all you want
but I was never waiting for your approval.
Sticks and stones may break my bones
but words will never hurt me.

Dreaming of something that may
never happen might seem silly to some
but for dreamers, all that exists in
this harsh reality are their dreams.
You take away their dreaming ability,
you take off their oxygen mask
to breathe and live.

Sometimes a stranger you meet
along the way captures your heart
more than a familiar one ever did.
I may never see you again but
after all they are all kinds of love
and you might be just for a night,
but will be remembered forever.

Every so often, even poetry fails to put the
depth and intensity of my thoughts into words.
I need several books, piles of words, long scrolls
to truly express what's going on in my mind.
Without the existence of poetry and words,
I have nothing to express myself.

Our society kills our dreams
and still doesn't let us be happy.
It forces us to bow down to their
so-called norms and do as their highness wishes.
I for one, refuse to let the society dictate my life.
I'll do as my heart wishes and go where the
wind will take my free soul.

Sometimes there are no words
for my thoughts; they choke inside
until they can no longer stay there and so,
they flow out into paper,
forming themselves into poetry.

And when the noise fades away;
there is utter silence in the background
and you can finally hear your thoughts.
There it is; a sinking feeling in your chest
that no matter how busy you keep
yourself during the day,
the truth is harder to escape at night
because the sun may see you during the day
but the moon knows all your deepest longings
and hidden desires for there is
no veil from the moonlight.

Maybe it's just not in the cards for me.
To love and be loved back till eternity
is a joy not granted to many.
I should just feel lucky to have loved at all
because no matter how overrated love is,
it still conquers all.

In all the hustle and bustle of people,
twinkling lights and smiling faces everywhere,
I feel all alone like a part of me is missing
somewhere and I am not able to find it anywhere.
That's the real tragedy,
feeling empty but not knowing
how to fill the emptiness.

In this world today,
everybody feels one thing and says another,
they keep their thoughts and emotions buried inside.
May be they are afraid of how will people respond
to it or maybe they are afraid of their own thoughts.
Whichever it may be, their true soul is in hiding from
the world and hence; it's not free to feel and express.
Don't cage your thoughts and emotions because
of any worldly fear. Let them out and just be.
That's how our soul is meant to be;
raw and uncensored.

I've come to the realization that it's not
the pain or our wounds that kill us but
false hope does; it plants seeds of hopefulness
till its rooted deep in our hearts.
But, when it fades far away
like a blurred dream there we are;
crushed from false seeds of hope.

I've always believed in the saying that our
tears were a silent prayer when no words
managed to come out of our mouths.
But now, I wonder what happens when even
our tears are dried from falling too much
and words are lost in our hearts.
All that we have left is pain and
aching misery in our souls.

Don't ever be afraid of being alone.
Take pleasure in your alone time and savor it.
Once you are comfortable in your own company,
you don't need another to make you feel at peace.
Because sometimes you need to spend some
time in solitude and enjoy being by yourself,
so that when you fall in love,
you don't do so as you are lonely but because
you are deeply in love with that person.

I sometimes wish that my life was like a movie
and whenever sadness would visit me,
I would sit and walk with it like a character
washing his pain away in the rain or while
looking down his window in a bus.
I would spend ample amount of time with my grief
till I was okay again and then at the right time,
I would bounce back with the perfect ending.
But, this life isn't a movie, we can't really choose
the timing of the beginning, the middle or the end,
all we can do is keep on going and never give up till
we get to our happy ending not a forever one,
but a real one.

This world is always rushing,
always in a hurry to be somewhere.
This made me think, does it ever stop
to take a breath of air. And it seems
that it does but not for long.
It only pauses and starts back again.
That's when it hit me that how it's said that this life
doesn't stop for your grief or your happy moments,
it simply goes on, I believe otherwise; it does stop,
if not for anybody else it does for you.
We are no good with suppressed sorrow
or repressed joy in our hearts, rushing through
life without allowing ourselves sufficient time
to feel what we are really feeling.
I say, feel your pain till it hurts no more and
enjoy the little things that make living worthwhile.
Just stop in your tracks and feel.

I feel more alive when I am by myself.
I can be who I am,
not what the world
wants me to be.
I am a lover of solitude
and a loner at heart.
I feel more like myself in my soul place
where my thoughts rest
and can wander as they wish.
Once alone, I get lost in a world of my own.

Beautiful human beings are not the ones
 with a perfect face or a perfect body.
They are the ones with a kind soul,
the ones with a pure heart,
the ones who understand instead of judging,
the ones who love instead of hate.
These kinds of people are rare jewels because
they are human, which not everyone is these days.
If you chance to come across such gemstones
in life, hold onto them and never let them go.

Deep Minds Anonymous

Sleeping at night doesn't come
easy to some of us.
Our thoughts are running wild in
our head and we can't give it a rest.
And until we are tired with our own minds,
and our inner world takes a break,
do we doze off into the world of dreams.
By then, the moon is fast asleep and
it's the sun that watches us sleep.

ABOUT THE AUTHOR

Madiha Batool is a poet/writer who pens emotions mixed with inspiration for her readers to savor and enjoy. A graduate with honors from a reputed university in her hometown Karachi, she majored in media sciences specializing in advertising and film making. An immensely talented individual Madiha has over 200,000 followers on her widely popular Facebook page Deep Minds Anonymous; besides being an extremely devoted daughter, sister and friend to her several adorable pets, she's an incredible cook, an avid reader and a classic film connoisseur. Drawing inspiration from life around her, Madiha balances emotion and spirit delicately in her poetry going on to soothe and urge the reader at the same time. For Madiha deep thoughts find their expression in words culminating in thoughtful poetry. The medium through which sincere and profound thoughts find comfort from their overwhelming selves is a passion for Madiha. Ideas and emotions that strike one in the darkest hours of the night are the insightful realities of life that she explores. This book is the summation of her earnest heartfelt poetry on the subject.